KELLY
Adam's Secret Dream

By Gary Bengston

Illustrated by
Harry Nelson

Copyright © 1991

PUBLISHED BY FIVE CORNERS DANFORTH ESCANABA, INC.
4897 Danforth Road
Escanaba, Michigan
49829

ISBN 0-9631057-0-1

Acknowledgements

I want to thank my wife Annis whose faith in me has
carried me through some rough spots and thanks to my daughters
Julia, Shelly and Ellen. Their encouragement has led me onward and upward.

Special thanks to my grandchildren, Adam, Brian, Kayela, Sarah, Alex and Shay.
If not for them the inspiration to write this book would have been missing.

Dear Kelly of whom this book is written--Rest in Peace, old friend.
You are still loved and missed.

Grateful acknowledgement is offered to Sandy Chapman for dotting
the i's and crossing the t's; for her long time support and patience.
I will always be thankful.

Harry Nelson -- his thoughtful and caring illustrations. Thanks Harry
for the numerous hours of specially colored dreams and the
talent for the communication of my desires.

Gary Bengston

As a release from his regular hectic business schedule, Mr. Bengston likes to spend time at his hobby farm/camp/cottage. Here he raises colorful golden, ring necked and oriental pheasants. He says that he feels "most alive and creative" in this setting, in and near the natural beauty of Michigan's northwoods.

In Memory of my parents,
Leonard and Evelyn Bengston.

It is from our parents that we inherit the right to dream;
not only of today but of tomorrow as well.
Because of these dreams, this book was written.

-- G. L. B.

KELLY

It seemed like such a long time since Kelly left. Kelly with the wonderful eyes. Summer had felt so good as Adam skipped barefoot through the warm, green grass with his best friend running next to him.

He never really noticed that Kelly didn't run as fast as he did the summer before or that he didn't want to play as long and as hard any more. It was just so good to be with him, sharing the beautiful golden sunshine of August with his best friend.

Then one cold, windy day in October, Kelly was gone. Adam tried so hard to understand that Kelly had gotten old and tired and had gone to sleep. He tried very hard to understand that his friend would never run and play with him on warm summer days again.

And then, when Adam had gotten about as sad as sad could be, he had a wonderful dream… in fact, it was probably the most wonderful dream anyone could possibly have!

One crisp, starlit December night Adam's mom was reading a Christmas story. He had a very hard time hearing what she was saying because his mind was talking much louder than his mother was! As he watched the sparkling snow on the ground outside of his bedroom window, he kept drifting away to a special place where he kept his secret dream.

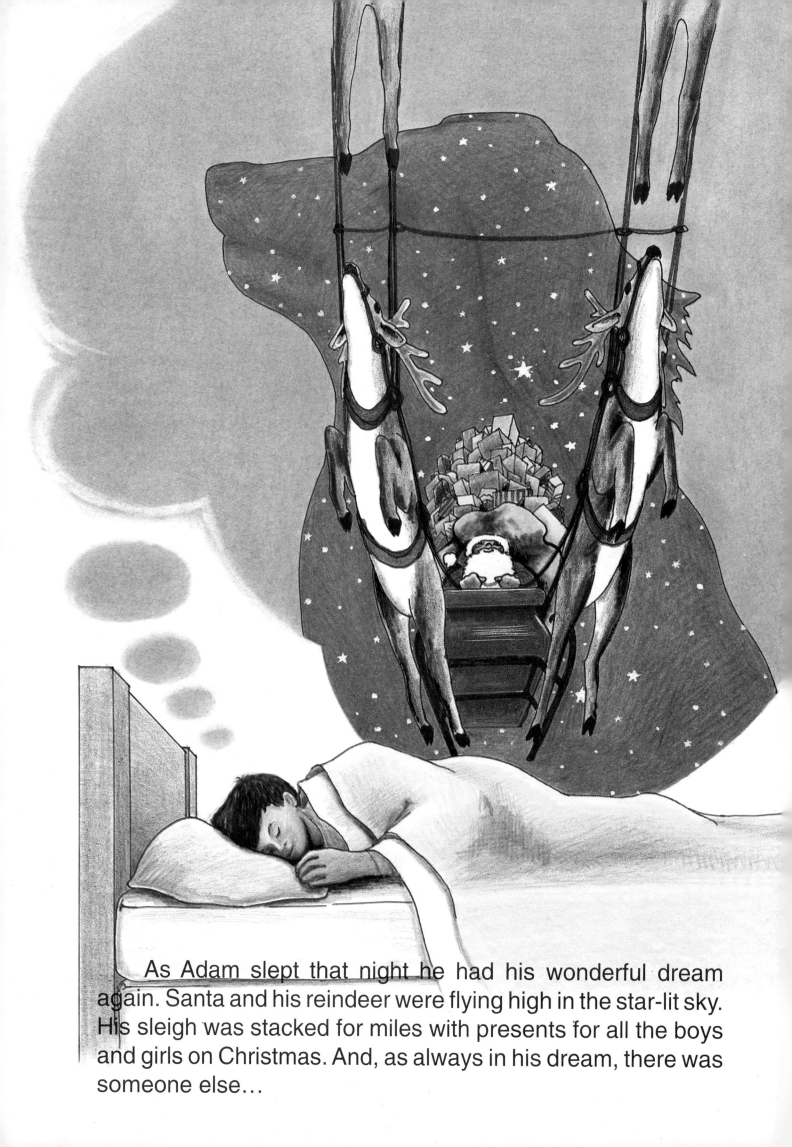

As Adam slept that night he had his wonderful dream again. Santa and his reindeer were flying high in the star-lit sky. His sleigh was stacked for miles with presents for all the boys and girls on Christmas. And, as always in his dream, there was someone else…

Adam was just beginning to give up on ever seeing another
weekend (the days were creeping by so slowly), when
Friday morning finally arrived.

During the day, Adam's teacher had to remind him to pay
attention to his work. But it was so much more pleasant to watch
the snowflakes drifting lazily past the windows while he thought
his warm thoughts, than to pay attention to math.

With every step Adam took on his way home from school, all he could think of was his wonderful dream. And he was very busy working on his "big plan."

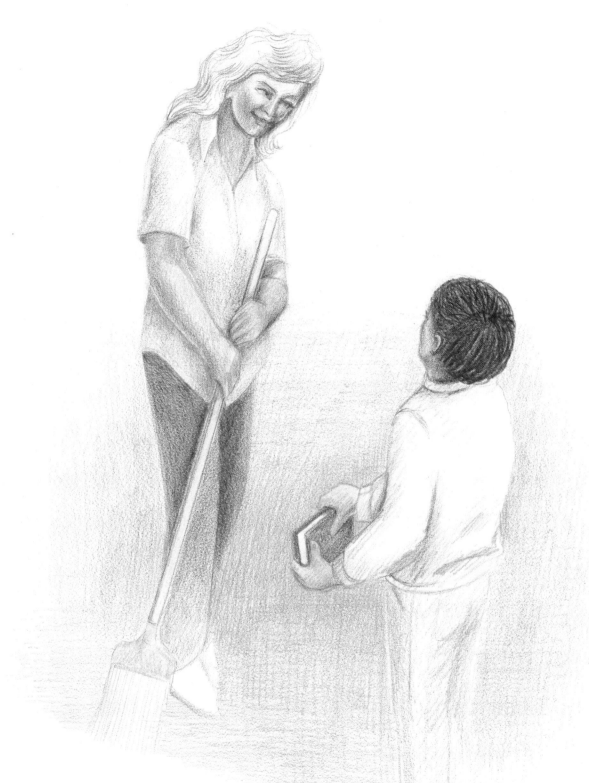

When he got home, he began to put his plan into action. "Mom," he asked, "are we going to Grandpa's store tomorrow to shop? I really need to talk to Grandpa." Adam's mom replied, "Well, let's finish the cleaning. We'll decorate the tree and wrap the presents. Then everything will be ready for Santa and we'll have plenty of time to visit Grandpa."

Adam worked very hard helping his mom. He also worked very hard trying to hide his growing excitement! One thought kept looming larger and larger in his mind. THIS DREAM COULD REALLY COME TRUE!

On Saturday morning, Adam awoke after a long, marvelous, dream-filled night. He was filled with man-sized thoughts about how his dream could come true and what he should do about it. He walked into Grandpa's store with big long strides, directly to the room where Grandpa was preparing meat for his display case. "Grandpa," Adam blurted out when he could stand it no longer, "I need a bone for Santa's dog!!" "So, Santa has a dog? And just how do you know this?" Grandpa inquired. "Grandpa, I really know that Santa has a dog and I know he'll need a bone for the long, cold ride back to the North Pole!"

Grandpa smiled a secret smile and chuckled to himself. He walked slowly over to a shelf, took the most perfect bone and handed it to Adam.

It really was a special Christmas Eve at Adam's house. On the kitchen table was a treat for Santa and his reindeer.

There was something for the special someone else, too,
and a note from Adam, that his mother helped him write. It said:

Dear Santa,

My name is Adam and I have been having a secret dream about your new dog. I hope you will enjoy the treats I left. I left a special bone for your dog. I know he will be hungry and cold.

Thank you, Santa

Love
Adam

When Adam went to bed on that shiny, sparkling night, he knew that everything was going to be perfect! He pressed his eyes shut and couldn't help the little shiver of excitement that started at his tippy-toes and ran in ripples up his body to the very top of his head. He grabbed his blanket tight and held it to his face so nobody could hear the tiny giggle that seemed to bubble out of him.

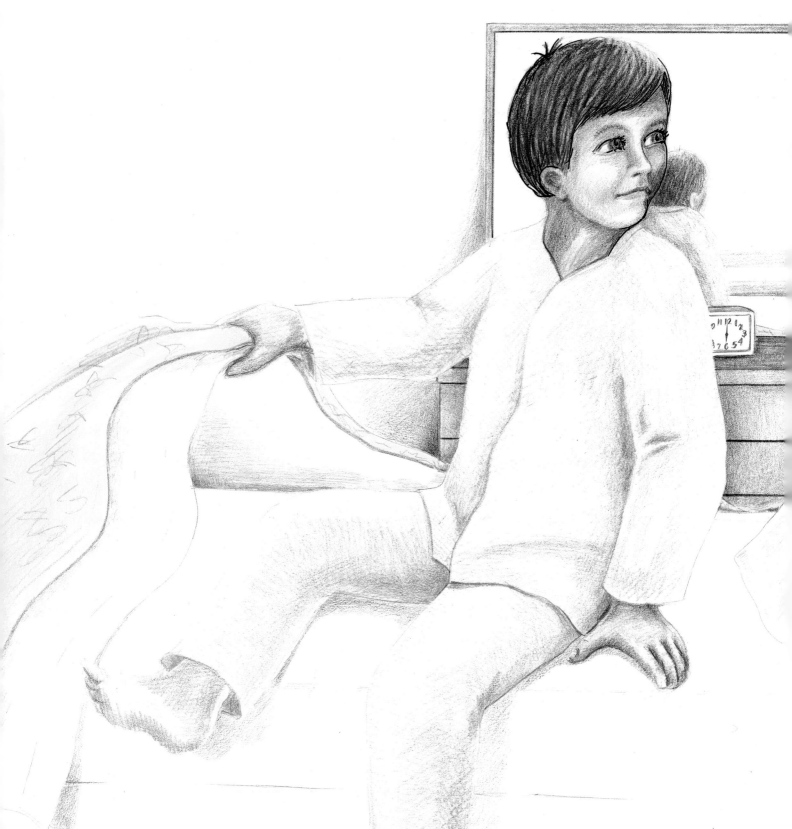

On Christmas Day, Adam opened his eyes just as a wisp of sunshine peeked through his bedroom window. He leaped out of bed, and almost before his feet could touch the floor he was through the door and racing quietly (so he wouldn't wake anyone) to the kitchen. As he stepped carefully through the kitchen door he held his breath. He could feel his heart beating as he slowly let his eyes travel across the kitchen table.

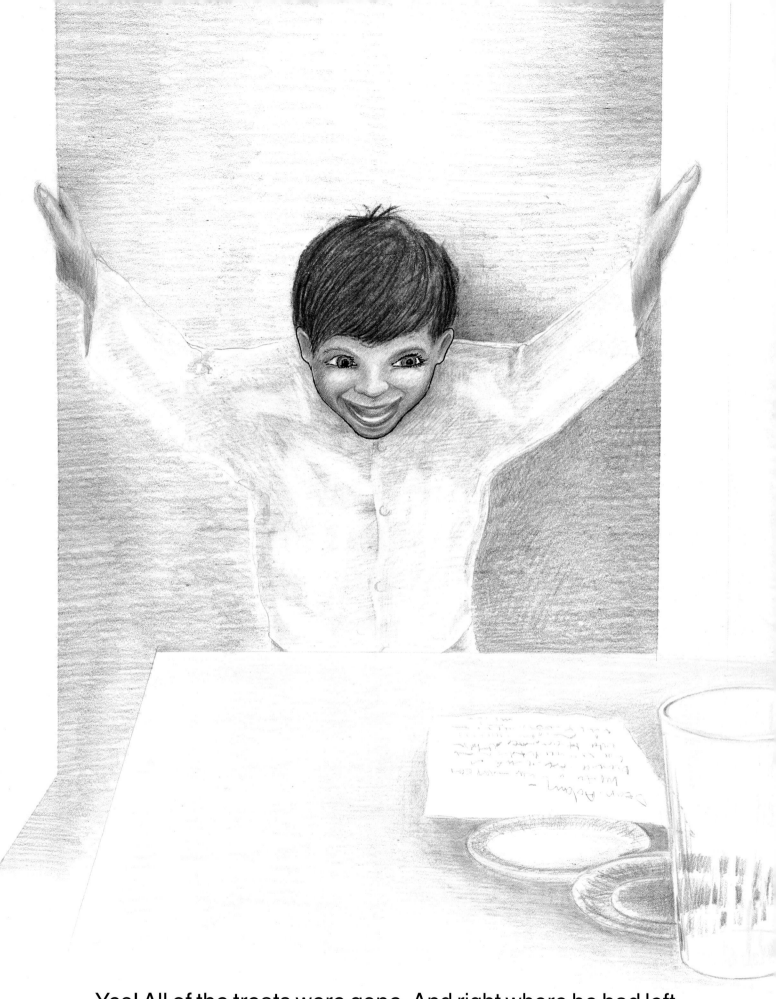

Yes! All of the treats were gone. And right where he had left everything last night, was a letter! He scooped it up in his hand, circled the table to gain momentum, and ran, as fast as his feet could carry him, to wake his mom and dad.

"Mom!… Dad!… Mom!… Dad! Santa took all the treats and left me this letter. Please read it for me… what does it say?" He was so excited! He had come to a full stop next to his mom and dad's bed yet his feet were shifting quickly from side to side as if he was still running.

It took Adam's mom a little while to figure out exactly what was happening. And Adam's dad breathed a very big sigh of relief to discover that there wasn't a fire, or that nobody was hurt. Adam's mom began to read:

Dear Adam,

Thank you for all the treats you left. We really needed them. It has been an extra long and cold night. We didn't leave the North Pole until nine o'clock and already we're a few hours late. We have a really large load this year and more homes to stop at than usual.

Tell your mom that I'm sorry for taking the afghan from the couch. I didn't think your family would mind because I really needed it. I have a new passenger in the sleigh with me this year.

I had been sitting back, enjoying my ride from the North Pole, and telling the reindeer we had to hurry. After a few hours of traveling, the reindeer made a swift turn, and no matter what I said, they would not change back on course with the sleigh! Suddenly we landed. And right along side of us appeared a wonderful dog!!

It was such a nice surprise to land at your house and find that you had left snacks for us and a bone for my new friend. How did you know what we needed? When I saw your mom's afghan, I wrapped my new dog in it right away to keep him warm.

The reindeer really like their new pal and take very good care of him. They are anxious to get home to show him to Mrs. Claus. He is a very special dog, Adam. He is black and white and very soft. But this is what makes him so special. He has one blue eye and one brown eye!

I am so glad you had that special dream, Adam. I have named my dog Kelly and I am quite sure that you already know him. I also know that Kelly will always love his bone treats as much as my reindeer and I enjoy the treats you leave us each year.

A Very Special Merry Christmas!

From, Santa, The Reindeer, and Kelly

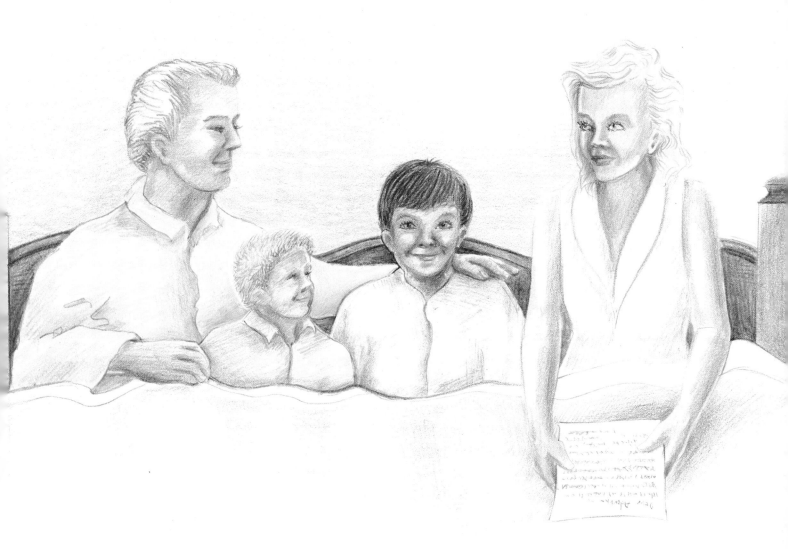

When Adam's mom finished the letter, nobody said anything for what seemed a very, very long time.

Like waking from a dream, they all seemed to realize at once what day this was and what they should be doing!

Now, Christmas Day for Adam's family was a very busy one filled with surprises. All the aunts and uncles and cousins would gather at Grandma and Grandpa's house. Their home was always warm and cozy and filled with the most delightful sights, sounds and spicy good smells of the Holidays.

There were stockings overflowing with treats and a wonderful tree with mounds of presents stacked in small sky-scraper piles beneath it. Didn't the tree seem brighter than ever before? Adam couldn't remember when it looked more beautiful.

All the grandchildren gathered in the living room, their eyes growing larger with every move Grandma made toward the six very overstuffed stockings.

"Kayela, Sarah," Grandma called, turning with a luscious Christmas stocking in each hand for two very Christmas-bubbly sisters. Two more stockings, "Adam and Brian." The last two were for Baby Alex and Baby Shay.

After all the gifts had been given, and everyone was enjoying what Santa had brought them, Adam began to tell everyone about his dream, Santa's note, the special treat he had left and the mysterious disappearance of mom's afghan.

But mostly, he told everyone about Kelly. Kelly with one-brown-eye-and-one-blue, the magical friend, now gone, that had spent so much time in his dreams.

Everyone was so interested in Adam's story that they almost didn't notice the six identical boxes that had, it seemed, suddenly appeared amid the shredded Christmas wrappings and torn ribbons.

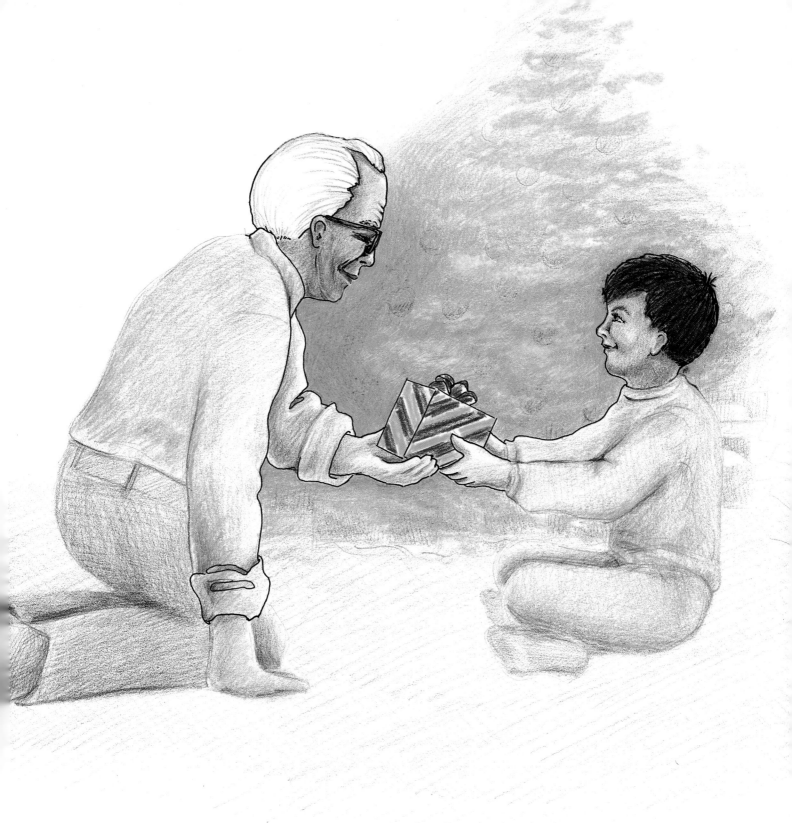

Grandpa got up from his chair and picked up one of the boxes. "This is a very special Christmas," he said, handing the first box to Adam. He then gave each grandchild one of the boxes. Adam, being the oldest and strongest, opened his first.

His mouth dropped open and you could see the tiniest tear
sneak out of the corner of his eye and trickle slowly down his
cheek. "A very, very special Christmas, Grandpa," Adam said
quietly. He reached in the box and lifted out a cuddly black and
white puppy, cradled in a small afghan. He cupped the puppy's
chin in his hand gently and lifted the little face to see what he
knew he would find. Looking up at him with a soft, unwavering
gaze, were two marvelous eyes – one blue and one brown.

Adam's Grandpa picked up a piece of paper he found in the puppy's box and began to read:

Dear Adam,

    I knew your Grandpa would choose the package containing the note. There are just so many mysterious and wonderful things about Christmas — and because of your special dream this has been one of the very best ever!

    Kelly has quickly become a special friend to all of us here at the North Pole. Because of him we will always remember you and your family at Christmas time. And I promise that no one up here will ever forget the marvelous story of <u>Kelly, Adam's Secret Dream</u> and how it came true.

Love,

Santa